A MUPPET™ PICTURE READER

Miss Piggy Camps Out

Written by Lara Rice
Illustrated by Rick Brown

©2005 Jim Henson Productions, Inc. All rights reserved. No part of this book may be reproduced or copied in
owner. MUPPET PRESS, MUPPETS, and character names
ns, Inc. ISBN: 1-59226-212-0. Printed in China.

reet, New York, New York, 10011.

 was picking .

She saw

and in a .

"Yoo-hoo!"  said.

"Where are you going?"

"To camp out,"

 said.

"Ooh! I love

to camp out,"

 said.

"May I come too?"

"Well...OK," said.

So  went in

to pack her .

 packed

a fancy

and fancy .

She packed a fancy

and a fancy .

She packed

a big box of .

Soon her was full.

 put on

her dark

and her best .

"I am ready!"

 said.

drove the

to the lake.

 pointed to a .

"That is a good spot,"

 said.

At the lake,

 and got lots of .

 sat in the .

"It is fun to catch ,"

 said.

Later, and

cooked out over a .

 sat on a 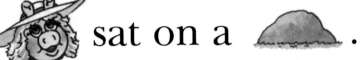.

"It is fun to cook out,"

 said.

The  went down.

The came out.

 and put up

their  .

"It is time to sleep.

 , where is

your  ?" said.

"  ?" said.

"I do not have a  !

I do not want a  !

I want a  !

A fancy  !"

 said.

And she called a  .

 got in

the 🚕 .

The 🚕

took 🐷

to a hotel.

"It is fun to camp out,"
 said.

flowers	Miss Piggy
Fozzie	Kermit
bag	car
gloves	dress

fan	pillow
glasses	candy
tree	hat
boat	fish

rock	fire
stars	sun
bed	tent
book	taxi